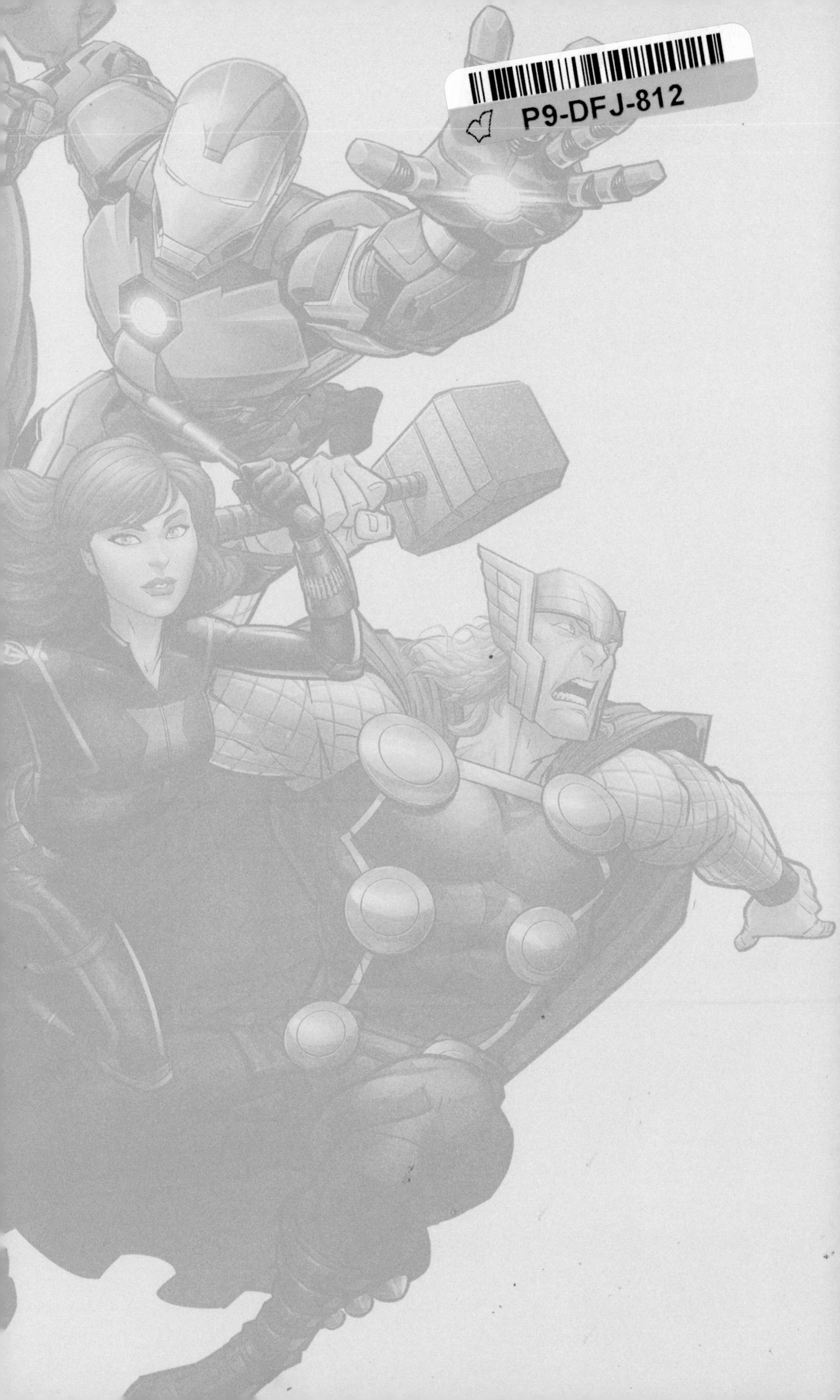

A LEVEL FOR EVERY READER

This book is a part of an exciting four-level reading series to support children in developing the habit of reading widely for both pleasure and information. Each book is designed to develop a child's reading skills, fluency, grammar awareness and comprehension in order to build confidence and enjoyment when reading.

Ready for a Level 3 (Beginning to Read Alone) book
A child should:

- be able to read many words without needing to stop and break them down into sound parts.
- read smoothly, in phrases and with expression, and at a good pace.
- self-correct when a word or sentence doesn't sound right or doesn't make sense.

A valuable and shared reading experience

For many children, reading requires much effort, but adult participation can make reading both fun and easier. Here are a few tips on how to use this book with a young reader:

Check out the contents together:

- read about the book on the back cover and talk about the contents page to help heighten interest and expectation.
- ask the reader to make predictions about what they think will happen next.
- talk about the information he/she might want to find out.

Encourage fluent reading:

- encourage reading aloud in fluent, expressive phrases, making full use of punctuation and thinking about the meaning; if helpful, choose a sentence to read aloud to help demonstrate reading with expression.

Praise, share and talk:

- notice if the reader is responding to the text by self-correcting and varying his/her voice.
- encourage the reader to recall specific details after each chapter.
- let her/him pick out interesting words and discuss what they mean.
- talk about what he/she found most interesting or important and show your own enthusiasm for the book.
- read the quiz at the end of the book and encourage the reader to answer the questions, if necessary, by turning back to the relevant pages to find the answers.

Penguin
Random
House

Editors Victoria Armstrong, Clare Millar
Senior Designers David McDonald,
Mark Penfound
Designer Jon Hall
Pre-Production Producer Kavita Varma
Senior Producer Mary Slater
Managing Editor Sarah Harland
Design Manager Guy Harvey
Publisher Julie Ferris
Art Director Lisa Lanzarini
Publishing Director Simon Beecroft

First American Edition, 2019
Published in the United States by DK Publishing
1450 Broadway, Siute 801, New York, NY 10018
DK, a Division of Penguin Random House LLC

19 20 21 22 10 9 8 7 6 5 4 3 2 1
001-316432-Sept/2019

A catalog record for this book
is available from the Library of Congress.

ISBN: 978-1-4654-9057-5 (Paperback)
ISBN: 978-1-4654-9058-2 (Hardcover)

Printed in China

A WORLD OF IDEAS:
SEE ALL THERE IS TO KNOW

www.dk.com

Contents

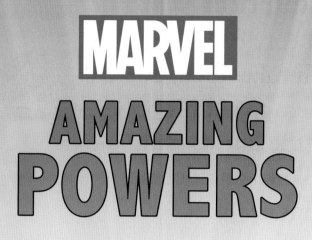

MARVEL

AMAZING POWERS

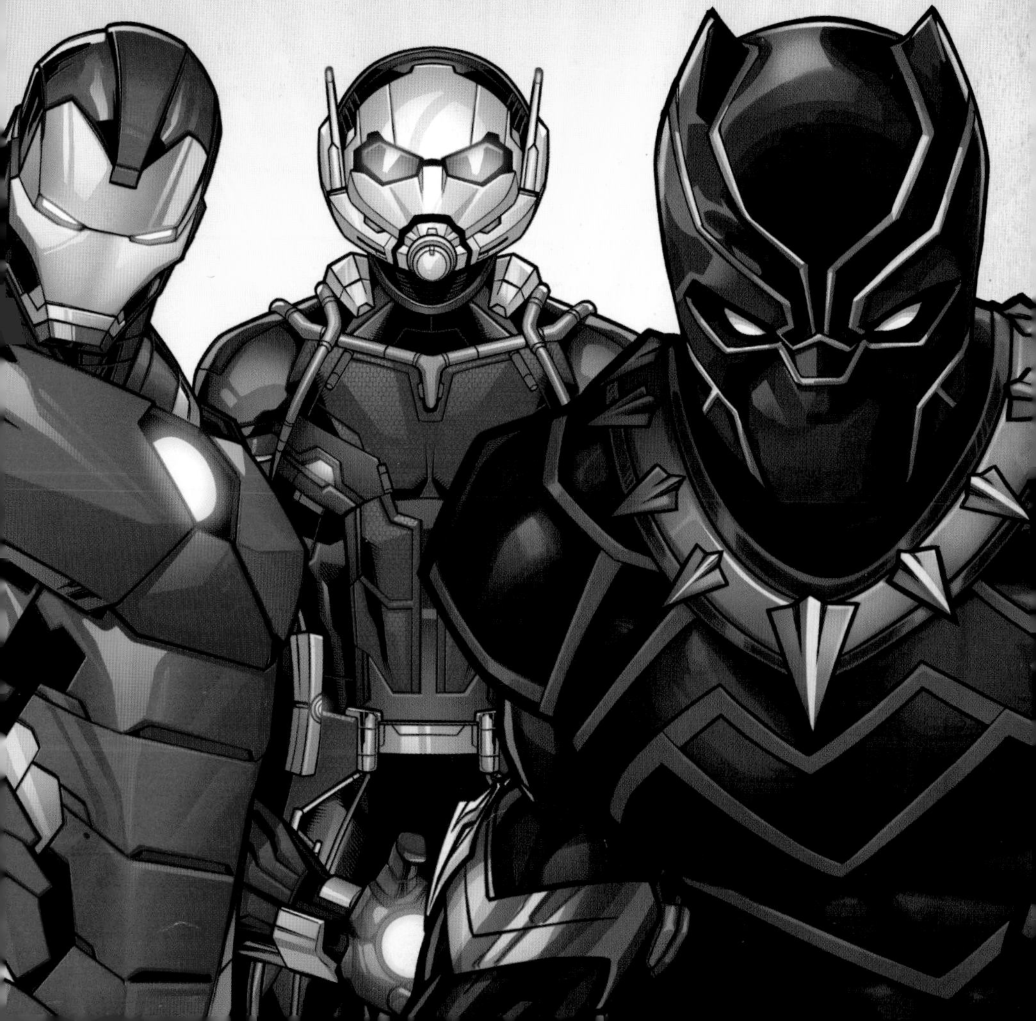

Introduction

It's not easy being a Super Hero. It takes great courage for a hero to put his or her life on the line to fight evil villains and defend innocent people.

But Super Heroes are men, women, and creatures with extraordinary abilities. Read on and meet some of the bravest Super Heroes around. Discover how they got their powers and find out how they put them into action!

But beware, evil Super Villains are always lurking just around the corner...

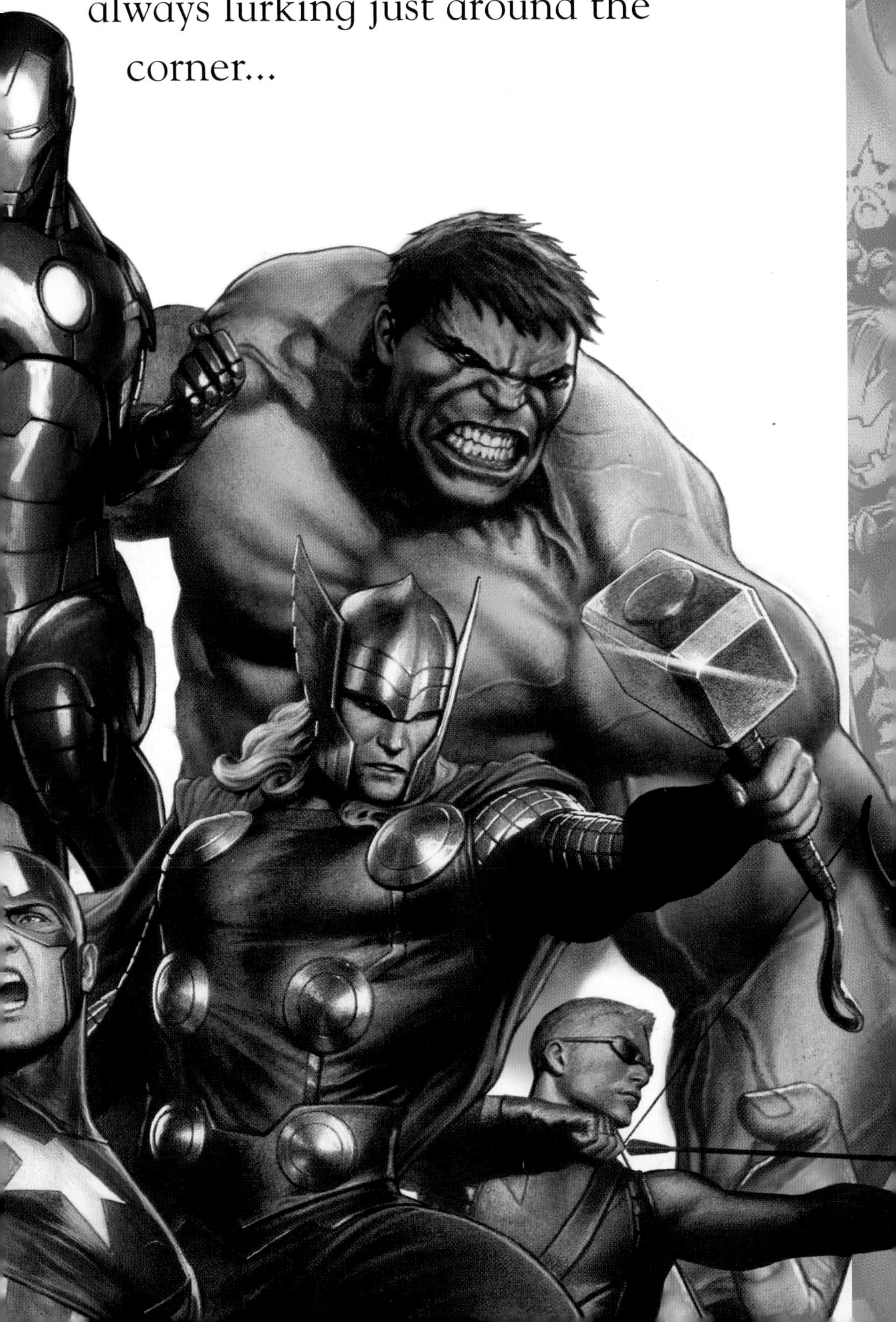

Spider-Man

Spider-Man is the secret Super Hero identity of high school student Peter Parker. While Peter Parker is shy, nerdy, and not very strong, Spider-Man is the opposite. Spider-Man is strong, fast, agile, and not afraid to take on bad guys.

Like a spider, he can stick to most surfaces which means Spider-Man is great at climbing walls! It's not just about being fast and strong, though, Peter Parker's brains are also useful to Spider-Man.

Amazing Accident
Peter Parker's life changed when he was bitten by a radioactive spider on a trip to a science exhibition.

The Hulk

When scientist Bruce Banner was caught in the blast from a gamma radiation bomb, it unleashed a whole different side to his personality. From then on, whenever Bruce becomes stressed or angry he transforms into the raging, unstoppable—and green— Incredible Hulk. Although his great powers make him very destructive, the Hulk really just wants to be left alone.

Super-Strength
Rage combined with gamma radiation gives the Hulk almost unlimited strength. His powerful legs can jump several kilometers and he can heal any wound almost instantly. The Hulk can even withstand bullets.

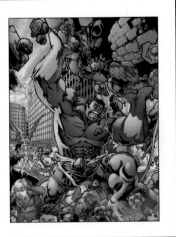

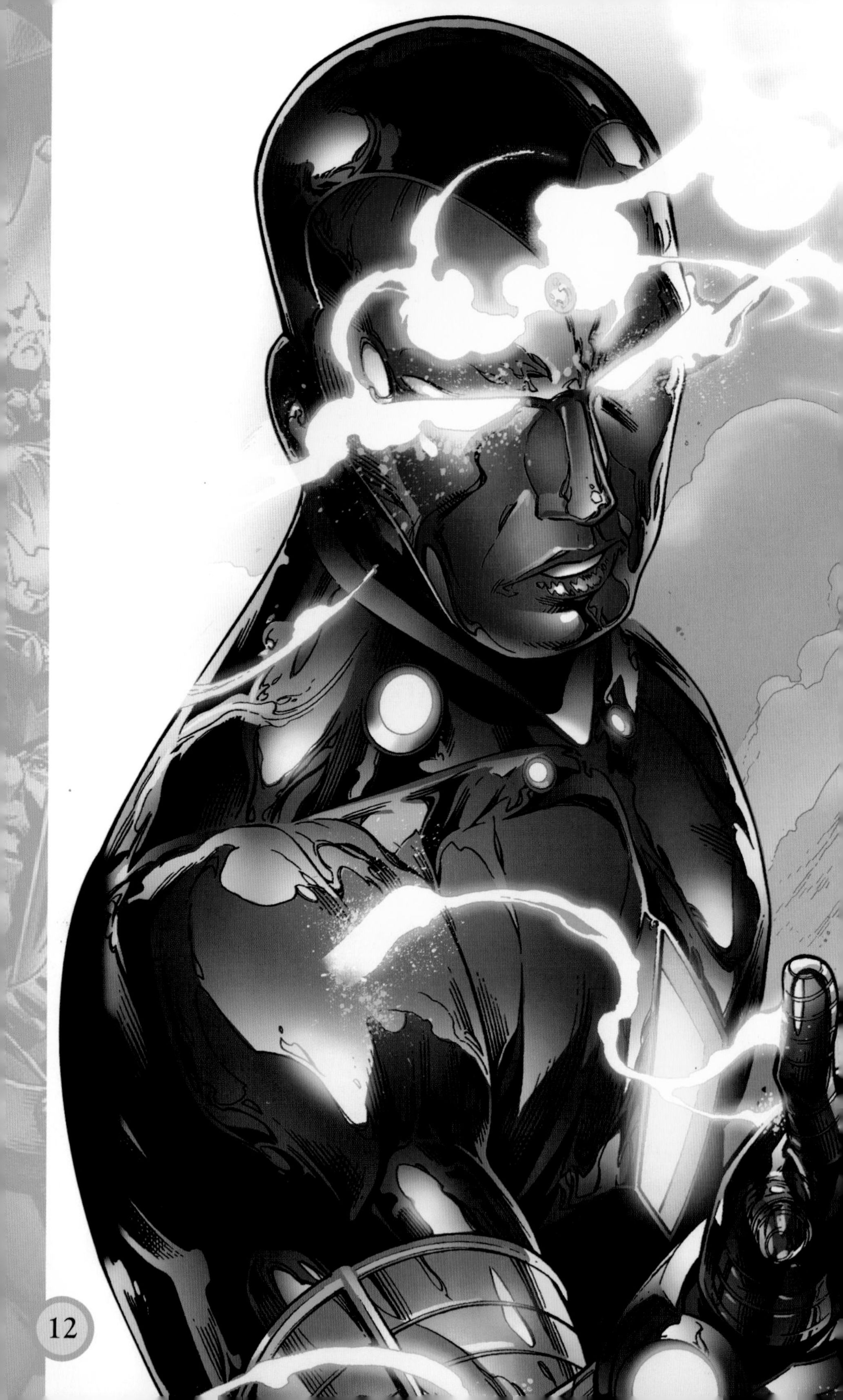

Vision

The evil robot Ultron creates an android called Vision. He is programmed to obey Ultron completely. Vision has some amazing powers—he can reduce his body's density so he is able to go through solid objects. This means he can walk through walls if he wants to!

He can also fly, has superhuman strength, and is able to fire bolts of solar energy from a device in his forehead.

Vision is not someone the Avengers want to have against them. However, Ultron is determined to use Vision to destroy the Avengers. Vision attacks the Avengers, but at the last minute, Vision turns on his master. He instead becomes a member of the Avengers.

Guardians of the Galaxy

The Guardians of the Galaxy are a gang of cosmic outlaws. They take on missions all over the universe and come to the Avengers' aid. At first, the Avengers aren't sure what to make of this wacky team. However, they soon see the Guardians' bravery when they help battle against the Super Villain Thanos.

Star-Lord is usually the leader of the group. Star-Lord is half-human and half-alien Spartoi. This brave leader wears a special helmet that lets him breathe in space. Star-Lord's Element Gun is his main weapon. It fires out blasts of the four elements: fire, earth, water, and air.

Thanos

Fearless Five
This brave team can
defeat any foe!

Groot

Star-Lord

Drax

Gamora

Rocket Raccoon

Black Panther

T'Challa is the king of the African country Wakanda and the Super Hero Black Panther. He is highly intelligent and a skilled fighter.

As a young man he attends top colleges and universities in America and Europe where he gains great scientific knowledge. Whilst traveling, T'Challa meets Ororo Munroe, who becomes his wife. Ororo Munroe is able to control the weather and becomes the Super Hero Storm.

When T'Challa returns to Wakanda he becomes Black Panther after successfully completing a series of trials. A herb, called the heart-shaped herb, gives him superhuman strength and speed.

Black Panther's suit is reinforced with Vibranium—a metal that is nearly indestructible.

Ant-Man

Hank Pym is a genius inventor.
He discovers particles that can alter
the size of objects and living things.
These Particles, called Pym Particles,
enable Hank to shrink his body to
the size of an ant.

Using a special helmet, Hank is able to talk to ants and becomes the amazing Super Hero, Ant-Man.

Janet van Dyne, Ant-Man's girlfriend, becomes Wasp and together they help found the  Avengers. Next to Thor and Iron Man, Hank feels very tiny so he adjusts his Pym Particle formula to turn into Goliath, at 7.6 meters (25 feet) tall.

Although small, Wasp can fly at speeds of up to 64 kph (40 mph).

Wasp

Janet, known as the Super Hero Wasp, fights evil alongside Ant-Man. Janet works with Hank to find the alien creature that murdered her father. Wasp shrinks to insect size using Hank's Pym Particles. She even grows tiny antennae allowing her to communicate with real wasps.

Wasp is able to fly at great speeds and shoots her enemies with electric blasts from her hands. She likes to confuse her foes by buzzing quickly around them.

Wasp helps found the Avengers and remains loyal to them, even when Ant-Man leaves the team.

The Avengers

A Super Hero team called the Avengers was brought together to defeat villains too powerful for a lone hero. The team was formed when Loki tried to take revenge on his adopted brother, Thor. Loki tricked Hulk into causing a train wreck, in the hope of trapping Thor. But instead, several heroes arrived to fight poor Hulk.

The group included Ant-Man, Wasp, and Iron Man as well as Thor. When they had defeated Loki, Ant-Man suggested that they form a Super Hero team.

The Avengers rescued
Captain America
and then asked him
to join the team.

Captain America

Steve Rogers wanted to join the US Army and fight in World War II, but he was turned down because he was too weak. However, when he volunteered to test the Super-Soldier Serum, Steve's body underwent an amazing transformation. It virtually doubled in size, turning Steve into a near physically perfect Super Hero with the ability to lift twice his own weight.

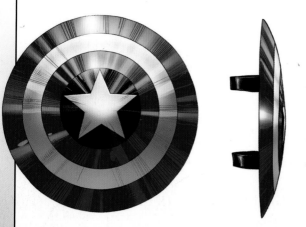

Tough Shield Captain America's distinctive shield is made of metal that is virtually unbreakable.

Now known as Captain America, Steve trained in martial arts, gymnastics, and military tactics. He has sworn to uphold freedom and democracy, either alone or with Super Hero friends.

Iron Man

Iron Man is the Super Hero alter ego of billionaire businessman, Tony Stark. Iron Man has superhuman strength and durability, thanks to his specially developed protective armor.

At first Stark only used Iron Man to deal with threats to his business empire but he later realized that his Super Hero persona could be put to better use. Iron Man became one of the founding members of the Super Hero team, the Avengers.

Weapons
Iron Man's armor has many state-of-the-art features. These include jet-propelled boots, gauntlets with repulsor beams, and a chest mounted uni beam.

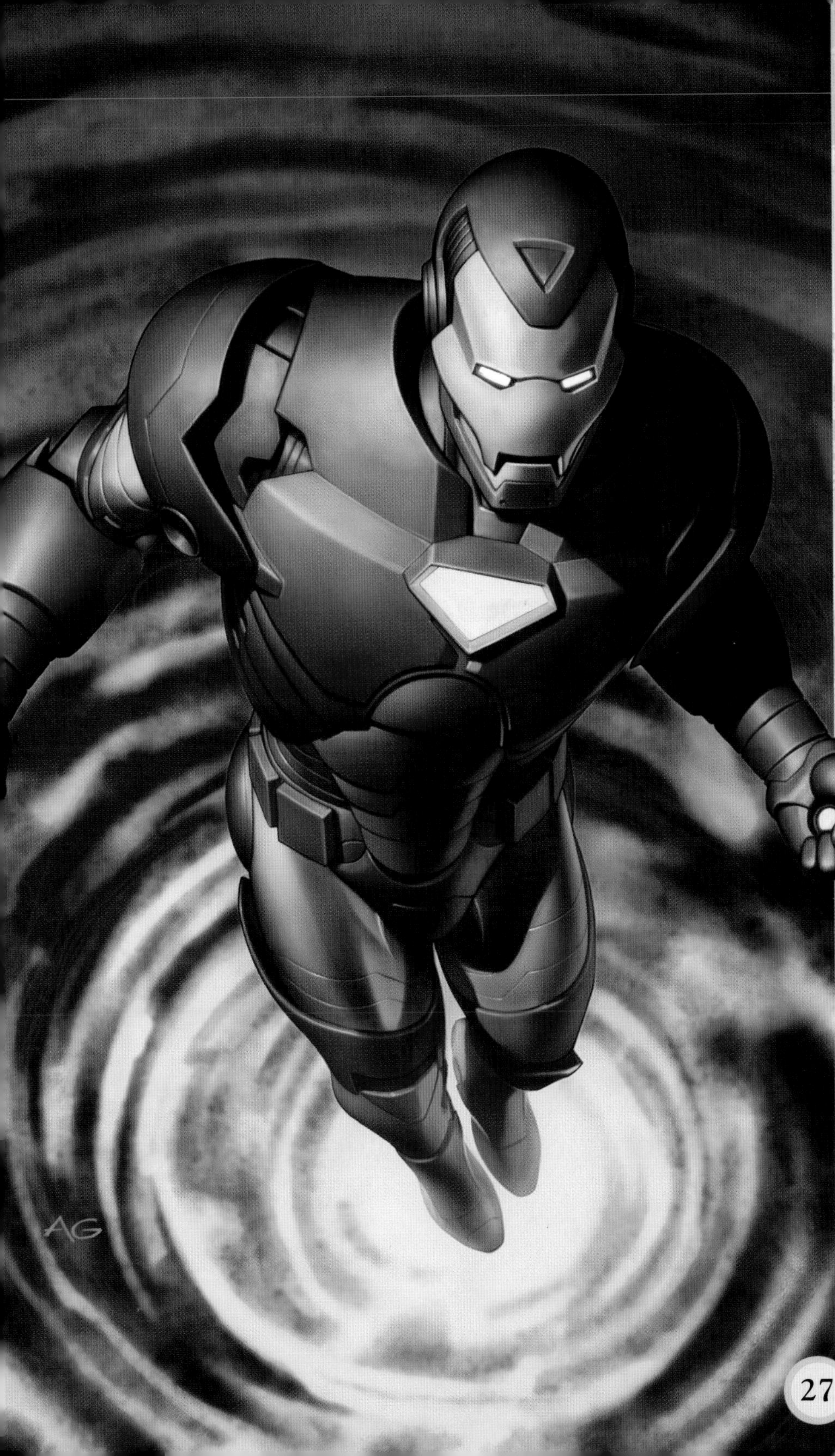
AG

Black Widow wears an almost bulletproof jumpsuit and carries many weapons.

Black Widow

An orphan who was brainwashed, Natasha Romanoff became a spy in Russia's "Black Widow" program. She is highly trained in martial arts and able to heal more quickly from injury than the average human.

Black Widow meets Hawkeye who decides to join the Avengers, persuading her to do the same. Once an enemy of the Avengers, Black Widow now uses her powers for good.

Scarlet Witch

An important member of the Avengers, Wanda Maximoff, known as Scarlet Witch, is one of the most powerful of all Super Heroes.

After Magneto rescues Wanda and her brother, Pietro, from an angry mob in their village, they agree to fight alongside him. They later desert Magneto to join the Avengers. They become known as Scarlet Witch and Quicksilver.

Thor

Thor is the Norse God of Thunder. His father, Odin, sends him to Earth from his home, Asgard, to become more humble. It's hard to be humble if you have awesome strength and are almost impossible to beat in a fight! Thor is immortal, like all Norse gods, meaning he will live forever.

Thor's hammer, Mjolnir, is made from a magical element called Uru. Thor can control the elements with Mjolnir, and summon it with just a thought. Thor is a founding member of the Avengers.

Thor's Hammer

Thor wields the hammer of Mjolnir. Not only is it unbreakable, but it can also fire energy blasts, channel storms, and open inter-dimensional portals.

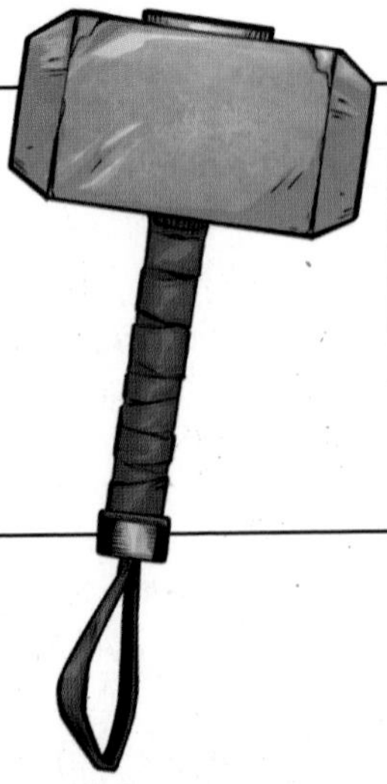

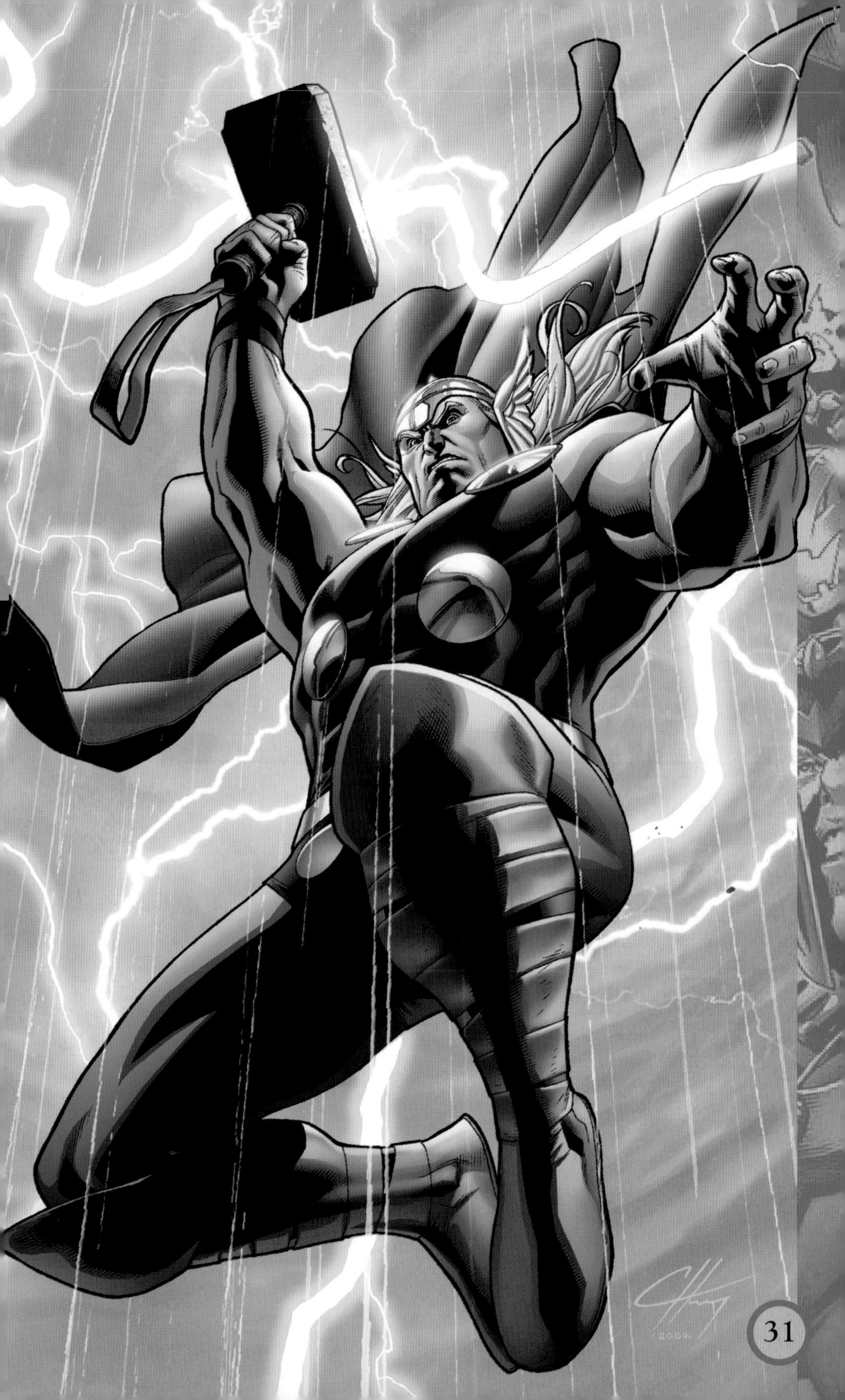

Namor

The amphibious Prince Namor
grew up in the underwater kingdom
of Atlantis. He is a super-fast swimmer
and can communicate
with marine life.
Namor also has
super strength
and stamina, plus
the ability to fly,
thanks to small wings
on his ankles.

Namor grows
weaker the
longer he is out
of the water.

Loki

Loki is the God of Mischief. He was adopted by Odin and is jealous of his brother, the Thunder God, Thor. He lives in the magical kingdom of Asgard.

Loki can shape-shift into any form he chooses. He uses black magic to play tricks and teleport across different dimensions. Loki is one of the Avengers' most serious problems—he loves to cause as much chaos as he can!

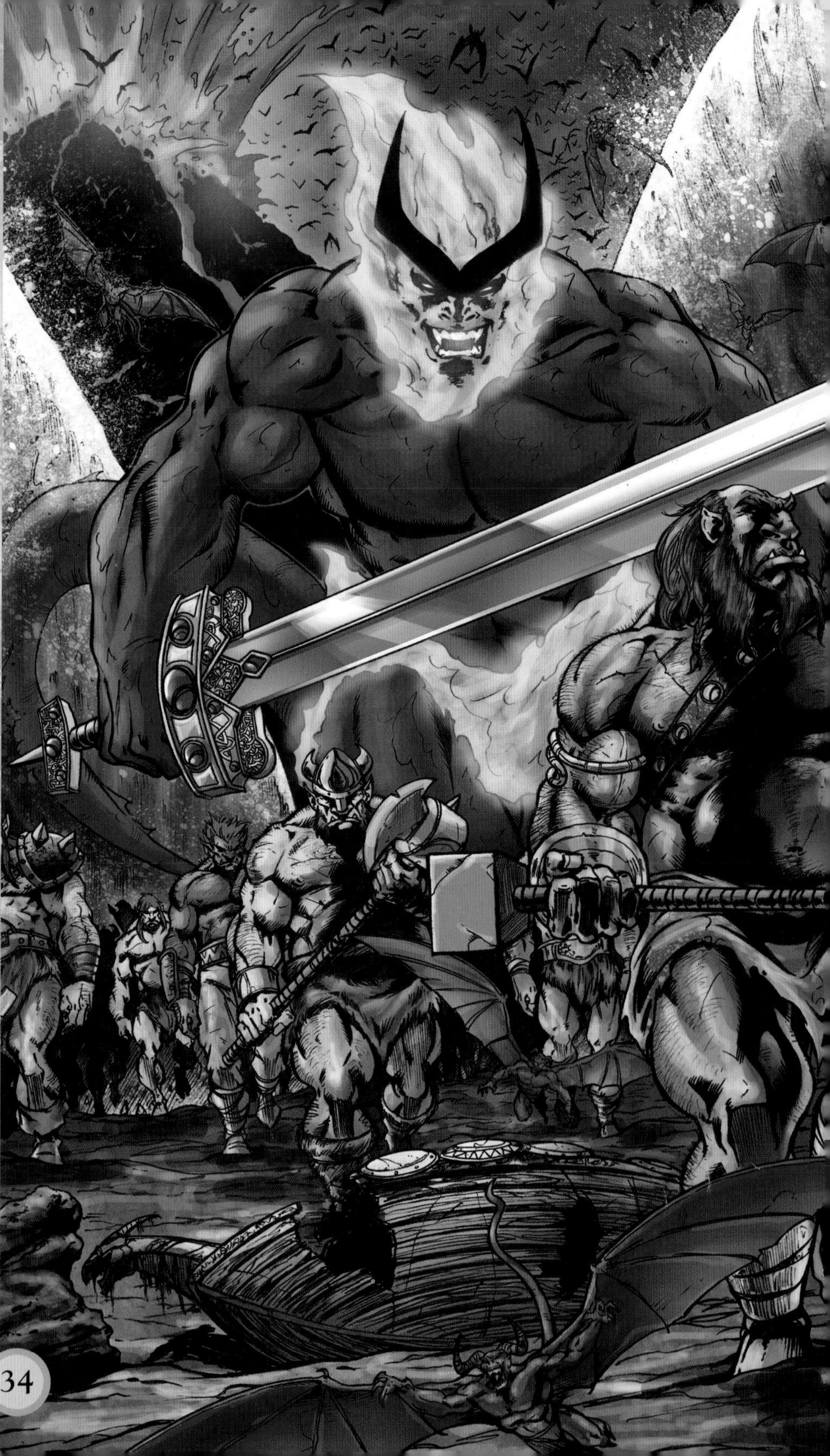

The Surtur Saga

Thor heard the legend of the powerful demon Surtur from his father, Odin. Surtur was a powerful force for evil who wanted to conquer Earth. When Malekith the Accursed opened the magical Casket of Ancient Winters, releasing freezing temperatures on earth, the time was right. With a sword mightier than Thor's magic hammer, Surtur broke free from his own dimension and began to attack New York.

Thor did his best to defend the planet from Surtur's forces, but he couldn't do it alone. At the cost of his life, Odin managed to send the demon back to his own realm.

Ultron

When Ant-Man experiments with robotics, he creates the evil Ultron. To Ant-Man's horror, he comes alive, escapes, and causes havoc. Ultron is one of the Avengers' greatest foes. Each time he is destroyed, he rebuilds himself to be even deadlier.

Thanos

Terrifying Thanos is another huge threat to the Avengers. Born on Saturn's moon, Titan, he is a sly and cruel villain. Thanos has a great deal of power, and is determined to rule the galaxy. Thanos craves destruction and wipes out many innocent lives.

Thanos is a scientific genius, and has created advanced and destructive technology.

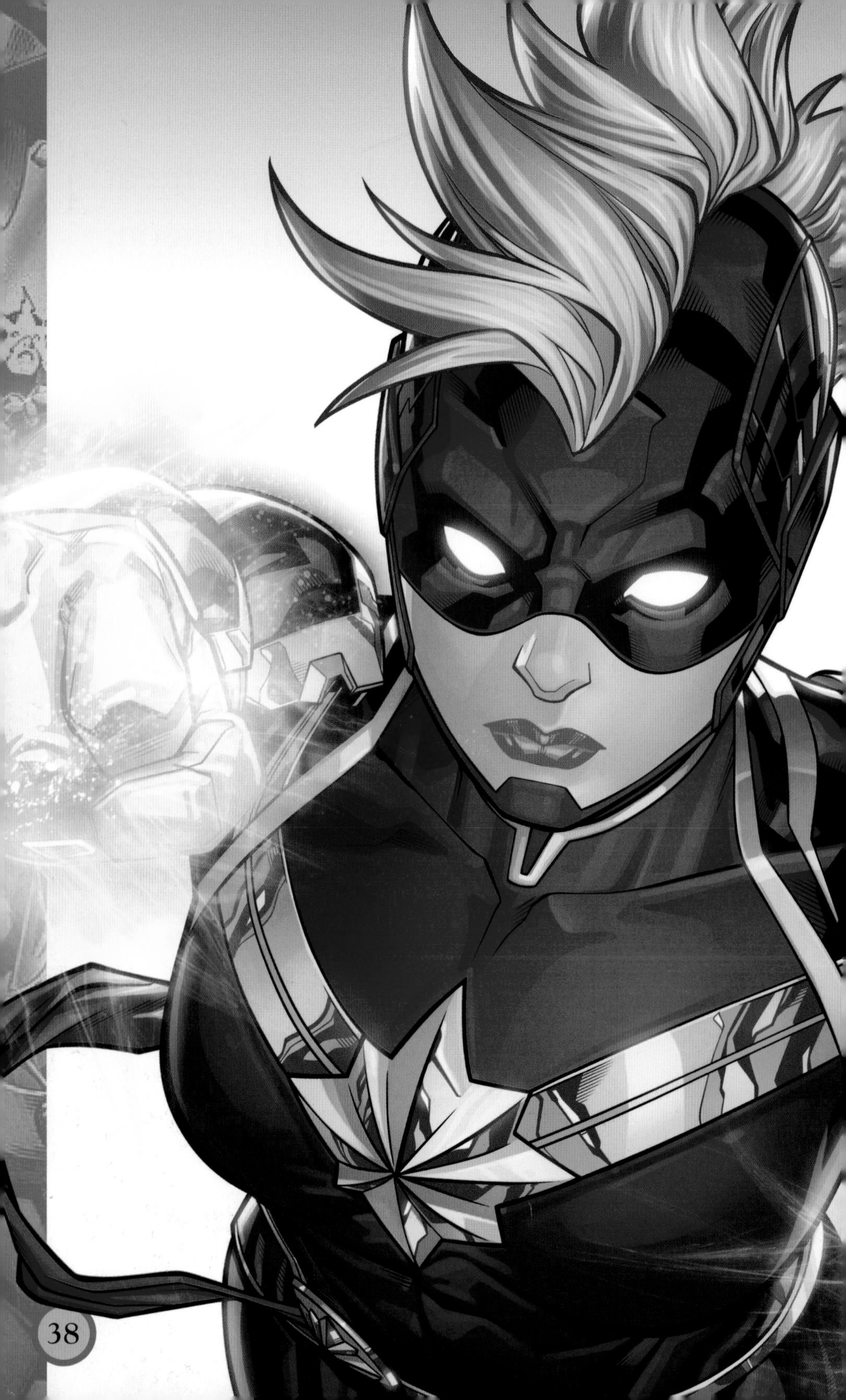

Captain Marvel

Carol Danvers gained superpowers after being caught in the explosion of an alien device. She now has superhuman strength and stamina. At first she was known as Ms. Marvel, but later decided to change her name to Captain Marvel.

Carol likes to work in a team, even though she can be stubborn. She was a member of the Avengers, and explored space with the Guardians of the Galaxy group. She even led an organization that protected Earth from extraterrestrials.

When she isn't firing energy blasts from her hands or flying, she is a writer, and lives with her alien cat, Chewie.

Road to Civil War

Captain America and Iron Man had
been friends and close allies ever since
the early days of the Avengers. But that
was before the government passed the
Superhuman Registration Act. The
act made it illegal for costumed heroes
to continue their wars on crime without
first revealing their identities to
the government.

With a firm belief in freedom of choice, Captain America opposed the act and became a fugitive from the law. Iron Man saw the act as the next logical step in fighting crime, and revealed his identity. The government then enlisted him to arrest Captain America and all who refused to comply with the act.

The battle lines were drawn.

Civil War

Captain America formed an underground resistance to oppose the government and the Superhuman Registration Act. Heroes such as the Falcon and Daredevil joined his cause against Iron Man.

Some heroes, such as Spider-Man and the Invisible Woman, switched sides in the heat of battle to join Captain America's forces. Eventually, Captain America surrendered, and ended the war.

The world is a different place after the Civil War. Some heroes work for the government now, and some remain in the shadows. But when there's danger, the differences fall away and they unite. It is simply what they do, because they are the Super Heroes.

American Hero
Realizing the fighting was doing much harm, Captain America turned himself in.

Quiz

1. Where was Peter Parker when he was bitten by a radioactive spider?

2. Who is usually the leader of the Guardians of the Galaxy?

3. Where is Black Panther from?

4. How fast can Wasp fly?

5. What is Iron Man's real name?

6. Who persuades Black Widow to join the Avengers?

7. What is Thor's hammer called?

8. Who created Ultron?

9. Where was Thanos born?

10. Who opposes the Superhuman Registration Act?

Answers on page 48

Glossary

Agile
The ability to move quickly, easily, and gracefully.

Alter ego
A side of someone's personality that is different, such as a secret identity.

Amphibious
Able to live both on land and in water.

Athletic
Active or gifted in sports, games, or exercises.

Durability
Ability to exist for a long time without deteriorating.

Endurance
The ability to withstand physical, and sometimes mental, pressures.

Enhanced
Increased or improved value or quality.

Extraordinary
Going beyond which is usual, regular, or customary.

Extraterrestrial
Of or from outside the earth.

Gauntlet
A protective glove.

Martial arts
Oriental forms of combat, such as karate. Martial arts can also be practiced as sports.

Military
Of or relating to the armed forces.

Opposed
To disagree with.

Radiation
Energy emitted in the form of waves or particles.

Radioactive
A way of describing an element that spontaneously emits rays that are often harmful.

Solar energy
Power that comes from the sun.

Stamina
Ability to sustain a prolonged stressful effort or activity.

Telepathic
The ability to read the thoughts and feelings of other people.

Vibranium
A metal that is nearly indestructible. Black Panther's suit is reinforced with this metal.

Index

Answers to the quiz on pages 44 and 45:
1. A science exhibition 2. Star-Lord 3. Wakanda 4. 64 kph (40 mph) 5. Tony Stark 6. Hawkeye 7. Mjolnir 8. Ant-Man 9. Titan 10. Captain America

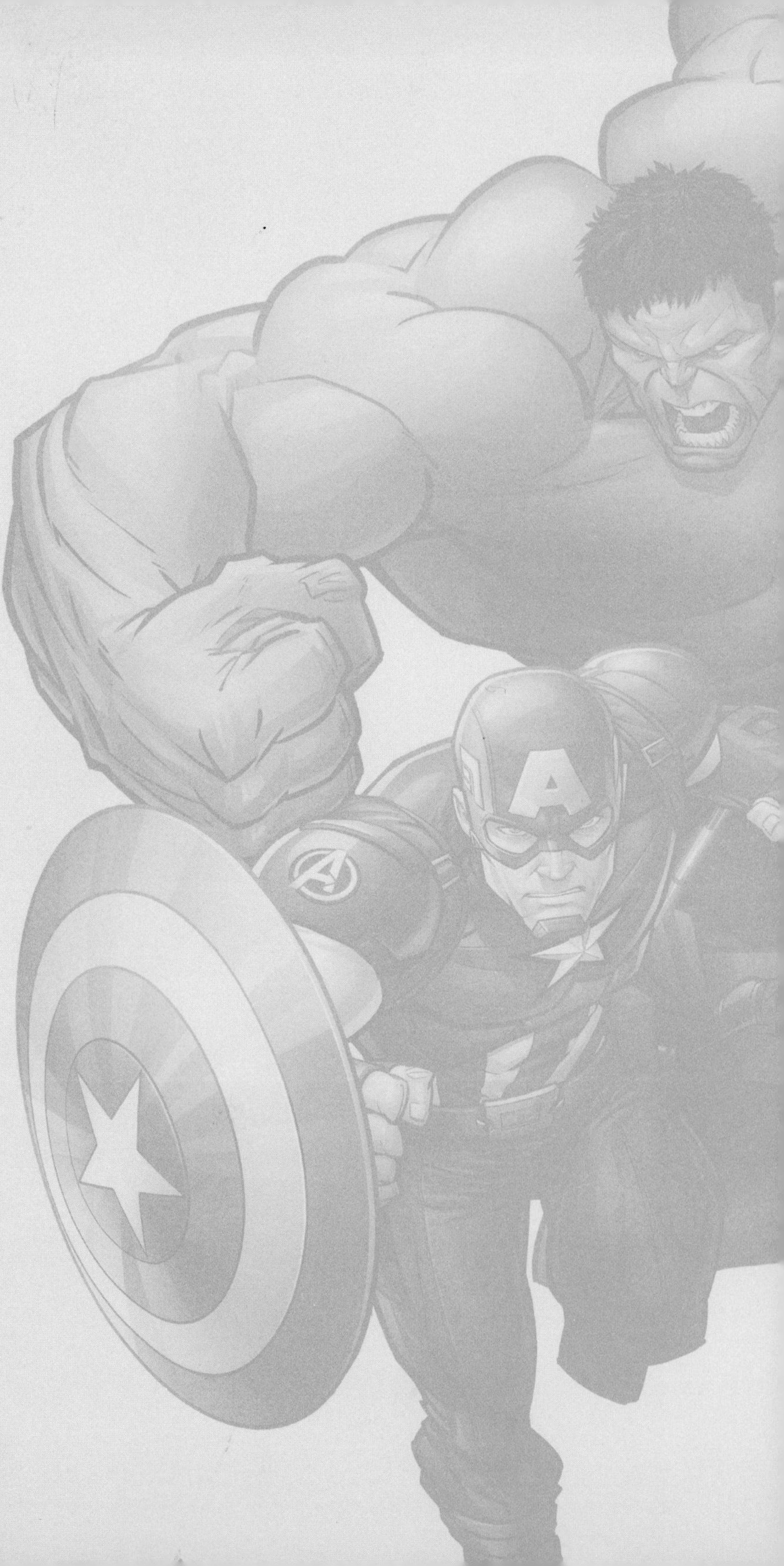